Gentry & June

A Story for Mom & Dad, Too

Tierney Boggs

WestBow Press books may be ordered through booksellers or by contacting:

WestBow Press
A Division of Thomas Nelson & Zondervan
1663 Liberty Drive
Bloomington, IN 47403
www.westbowpress.com
1 (866) 928-1240

ISBN: 978-1-9736-6050-7 (sc)
ISBN: 978-1-9736-6051-4 (e)

Library of Congress Control Number: 2019906875

Print information available on the last page.

WestBow Press rev. date: 06/06/2019

WESTBOW
PRESS®
A DIVISION OF THOMAS NELSON
& ZONDERVAN

Parents—If you see yourself in this story, consider answering the reflective questions following. And if you are craving additional inspiration, please read the letter following the questions. Hopefully this story, the questions, and the letter will give you a tiny boost of energy and perspective, enough to think a new thought or even take a new step. Adventure on!

Gentry has a best friend,

And her name is June.

June and Gentry.

Gentry and June.

They love to play

and learn and grow.

Eating ice cream, climbing trees,

being on the go.

Gentry has a knack for fishing.

June loves to watch the birds.

The lake is where they find adventure,

Where they feel alive, in other words.

On one of those long summer days

They imagined how it would be

If they had another friend to play with,

A perfect team of three.

So they went looking for a friend,

And when they saw him they just knew.

A puppy named Sam with brown, floppy ears,

It all felt so exciting and new.

And just like that, in one short moment

Their team of two was now three.

To their surprise their days looked quite different

Than they had imagined them to be.

Gentry and June walk Sam every day

Like all good puppy owners do.

And of course they feed him every four hours,

They pick up on his every cue.

But slowly and surely

Gentry and June forgot what they enjoyed to do.

They loved Sam so much and gave all they had

That they forgot to love themselves too.

One warm day they walked Sam by the path

They used to take to the lake.

And when they saw that grown—up trail

Their hearts began to ache.

They remembered the sweet taste of ice cream

And the tug of the line on the pole.

They forgot about their love for adventure

When they took on this new role.

So together they chose to make a small change,

And they took Sam to the lake.

Where together they bird watched, fished,

ate ice cream, and suddenly they were awake.

"Loving Sam does not mean forgetting

Who we are and what we loved before.

Just as we imagined, Sam can be

a part of our adventure;

He can make the adventure so much more."

And so then with one small change

They knew what they needed to do.

They chose to love their team of three

And to embrace all that was new.

And then from that day forward

Their three was better than their two.

The lake was more special than before,

And Gentry & June's love for each other grew.

Love the LORD your God with all your heart and with all your soul and with all your strength. These commandments that I give you today are to be on your hearts. Impress them on your children. Talk about them when you sit at home and when you walk along the road, when you lie down and when you get up.

Deuteronomy 6: 5–7

Questions to ponder

How can your children enhance your and your spouse's God-given adventure(s)?

What has been the best experience you and your spouse have had modeling your love for the Lord?

What made this experience the best?

What small step can you take toward bringing your children along on your journey of loving the Lord?

Dear adventurer,

Before you had little ones, did you and your spouse go on adventures? Adventuring with Christ was simpler when you did not have to bring a diaper bag and six different snack options. Does it seem you were running your race and when you had children, your race stopped? Have you ever thought, "As soon as they get older, we will start running again." I did, and I am here to tell you—don't stop running. Throw on your carrier and get your jogging stroller and bring those kiddos with you! I encourage you to keep pursuing Christ and your marriage, because we have a way of losing our identity when we stop running. I encourage you to see your children in a way that enhances this adventure. And as you bring your kids along on your journey, you may find they have a way of making it even better.

Deuteronomy 6: 5–7 assumes we don't just teach our children about our love for the Lord while we "sit at home," but we are also showing our love for the Lord when we walk along the road, when we lie down and when we get up. This verse assumes our child(ren) are with us always. AND loving the Lord doesn't mean sitting idle for an entire season of our lives. We are called to impress our love for the Lord on our children, modeling through our behavior through every step of our journey. "When you walk along the road" assumes you are moving, right?

In this story, Sam had the potential to add life to their life and adventure to their adventure. But in order to see that, they had to walk down their path. Don't sacrifice your path for your child's path. Teach them how to run their race by running yours. Don't forget your adventure for the sake of all the "shoulds" that come with parenthood. Run your race, live your adventure, and explore how your child can make your adventure so much more. I am curious—where is the grown-up path that leads to your lake?

CPSIA information can be obtained
at www.ICGtesting.com
Printed in the USA
BVHW021323190619

551410BV00015B/424/P

9 781973 660507